CB061758

TINO FREITAS • JANA GLATT

LITTLE STEPS TO A BIG HUG

Transcreation from the Portuguese
by Diane Grosklaus Whitty

PANDA BOOKS

© Tino Freitas and Jana Glatt
Translation © Diane Grosklaus Whitty

Editorial Director
Marcelo Duarte

Book and Cover Design
Jana Glatt

Commercial Director
Patth Pachas

Printing
PifferPrint

Special Projects Director
Tatiana Fulas

Editorial Coordinator
Vanessa Sayuri Sawada

Editorial Assistants
Camila Martins
Henrique Torres

CIP-BRASIL. CATALOGAÇÃO NA PUBLICAÇÃO
SINDICATO NACIONAL DOS EDITORES DE LIVROS, RJ

F938L
Freitas, Tino
 Little steps to a big hug / Tino Freitas, Jana Glatt; tradução Diane Grosklaus Whitty. – 1. ed. – São Paulo: Panda Books, 2022. 24 pp. il.

Tradução de: Um abraço passo a passo
ISBN 978-65-5697-124-7

1. Ficção. 2. Literatura infantojuvenil brasileira. I. Glatt, Jana. II. Whitty, Diane Grosklaus. III. Título.

21-72545	CDD: 808.899282
	CDU: 82-93(81)

Bibliotecária: Camila Donis Hartmann – CRB-7/6472

2022
All rights reserved to Panda Books.
A division of Editora Original Ltda.
Rua Henrique Schaumann, 286, cj. 41
05413-010 – São Paulo – SP – Brazil
Tel./Fax: (11) 3088-8444
edoriginal@pandabooks.com.br
www.pandabooks.com.br
Visit our Facebook, Instagram and Twitter.

No part of this publication may be reproduced, distributed, or transmitted, in any form or by any means without the prior authorization of Editora Original Ltda. Copyright infringement is established in Law number 9.610/98 and punished by article 184 of the Brazilian Criminal Code.

For Rita and Francisco, this book,
my love, and all my steps.
Tino Freitas

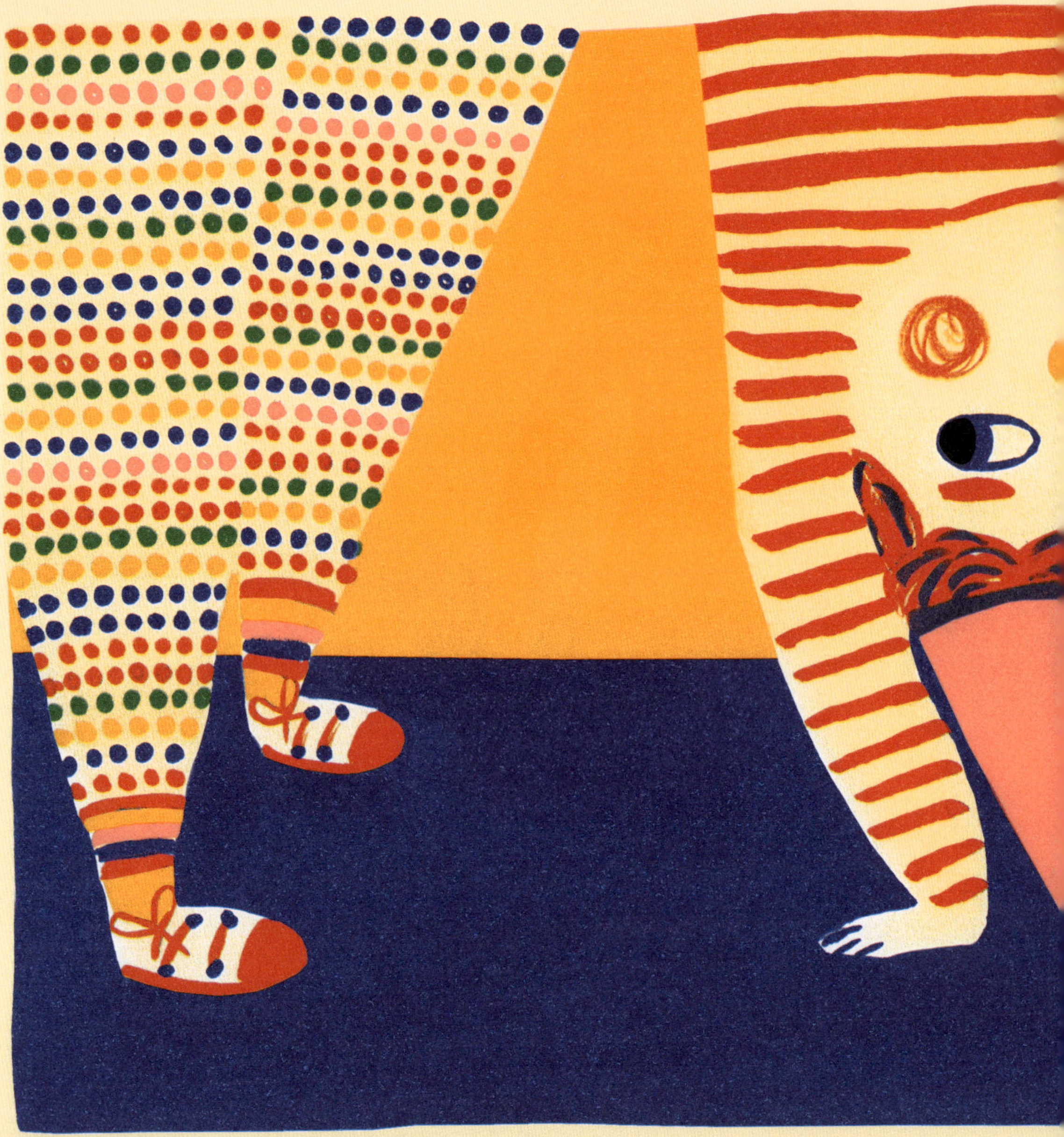

ONE LITTLE STEP,
JUST LIKE AN ANT.
MOMMY WATCHED
AND HER SMILE DANCED.

TWO LITTLE STEPS, JUST LIKE A CAT.
DADDY CALLED ME AN ACROBAT.

THREE LITTLE STEPS, JUST LIKE A FROG.
SISTER TOLD ME, "LEAP, DON'T WALK!"

FOUR LITTLE STEPS,
JUST LIKE A DUCK
GRANDMA SAID,
"I'M THUNDERSTRUCK!"

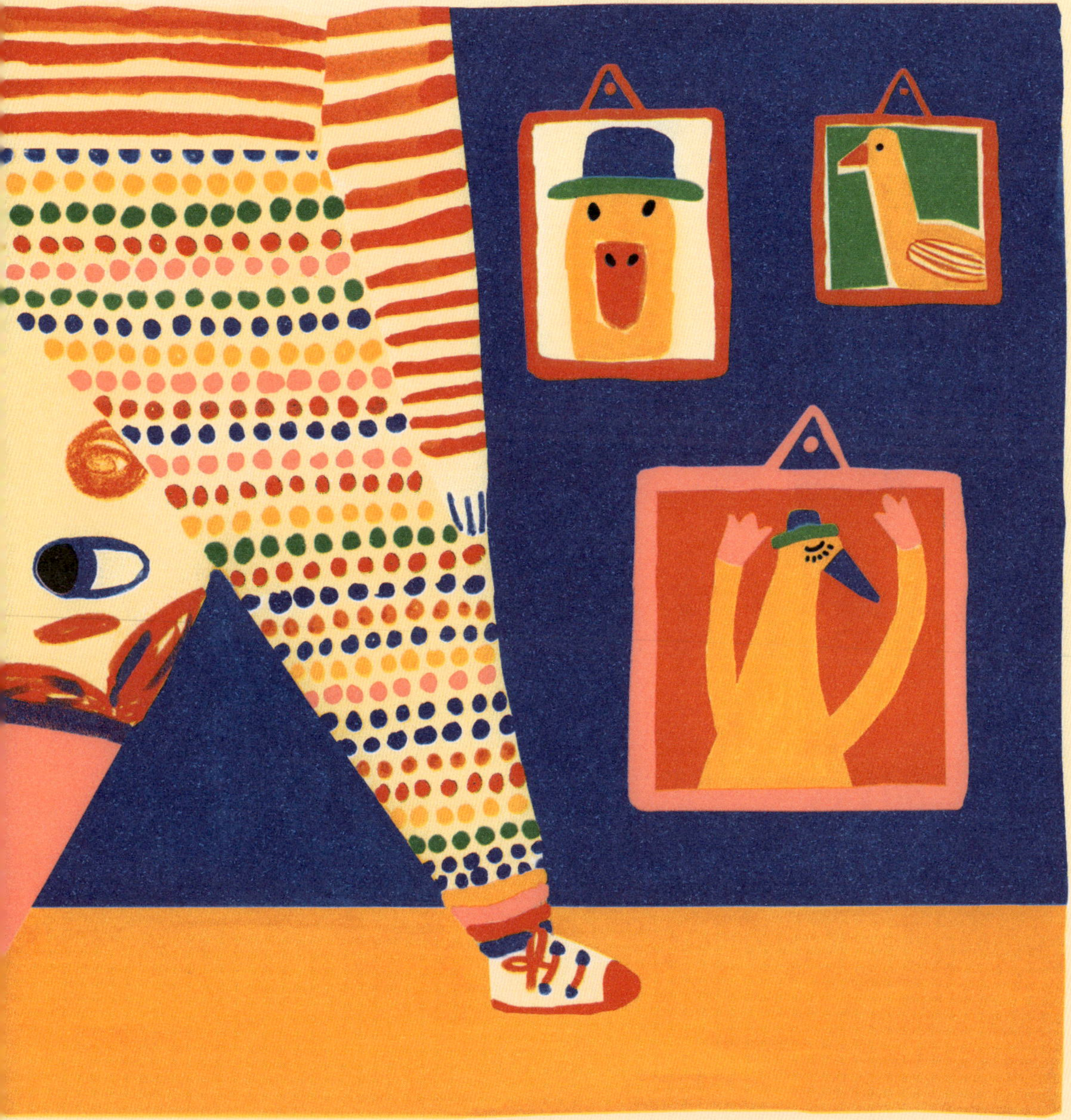

FIVE LITTLE STEPS, LIKE AN ARMADILLO.
"BOW WOW WOW," SAID OUR PUPPY WILLOW.

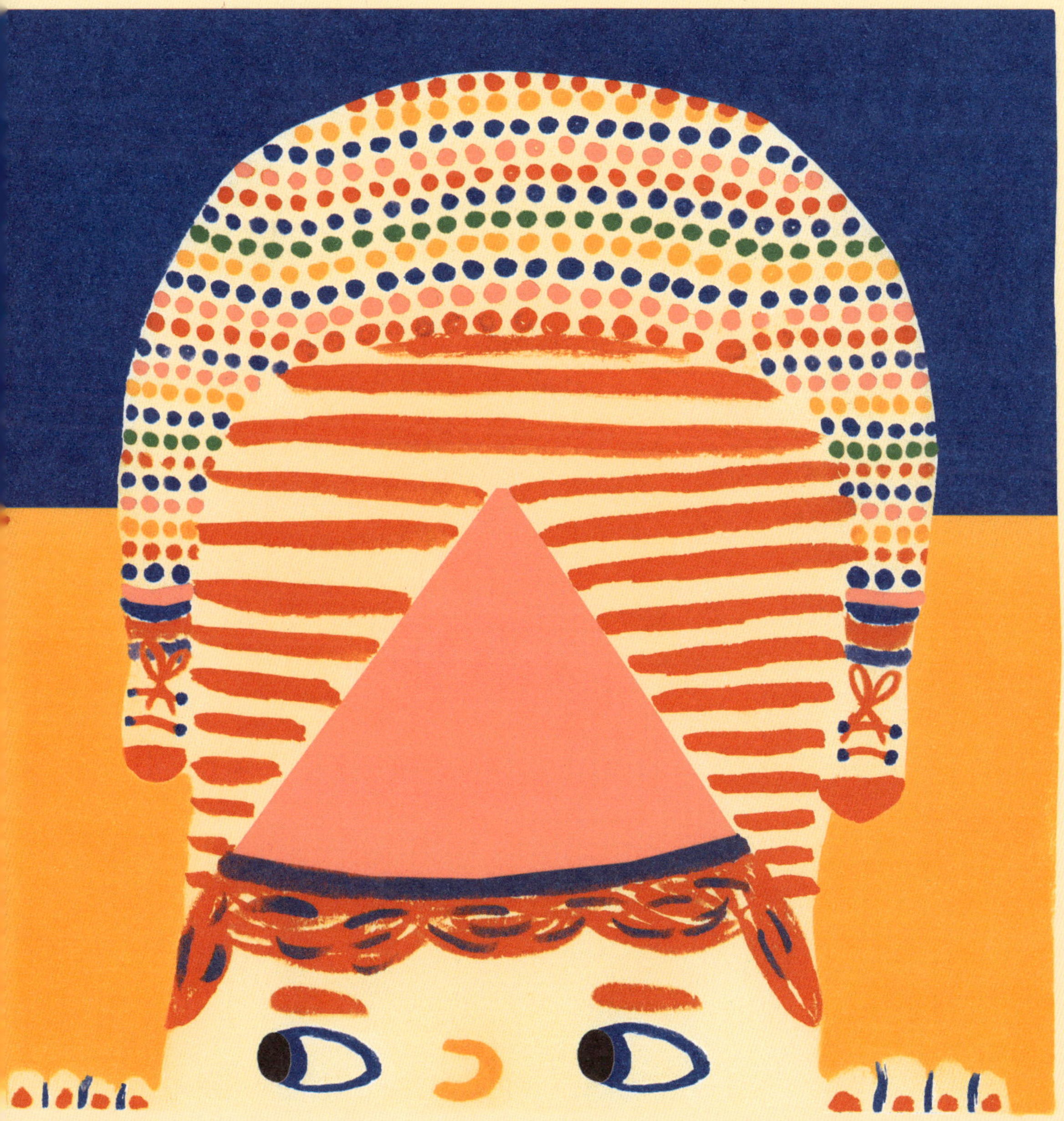

SIX LITTLE STEPS, LIKE AN OLD T-REX.
MOMMY'S FRIEND SAID, "YOU'RE THE BEST!"

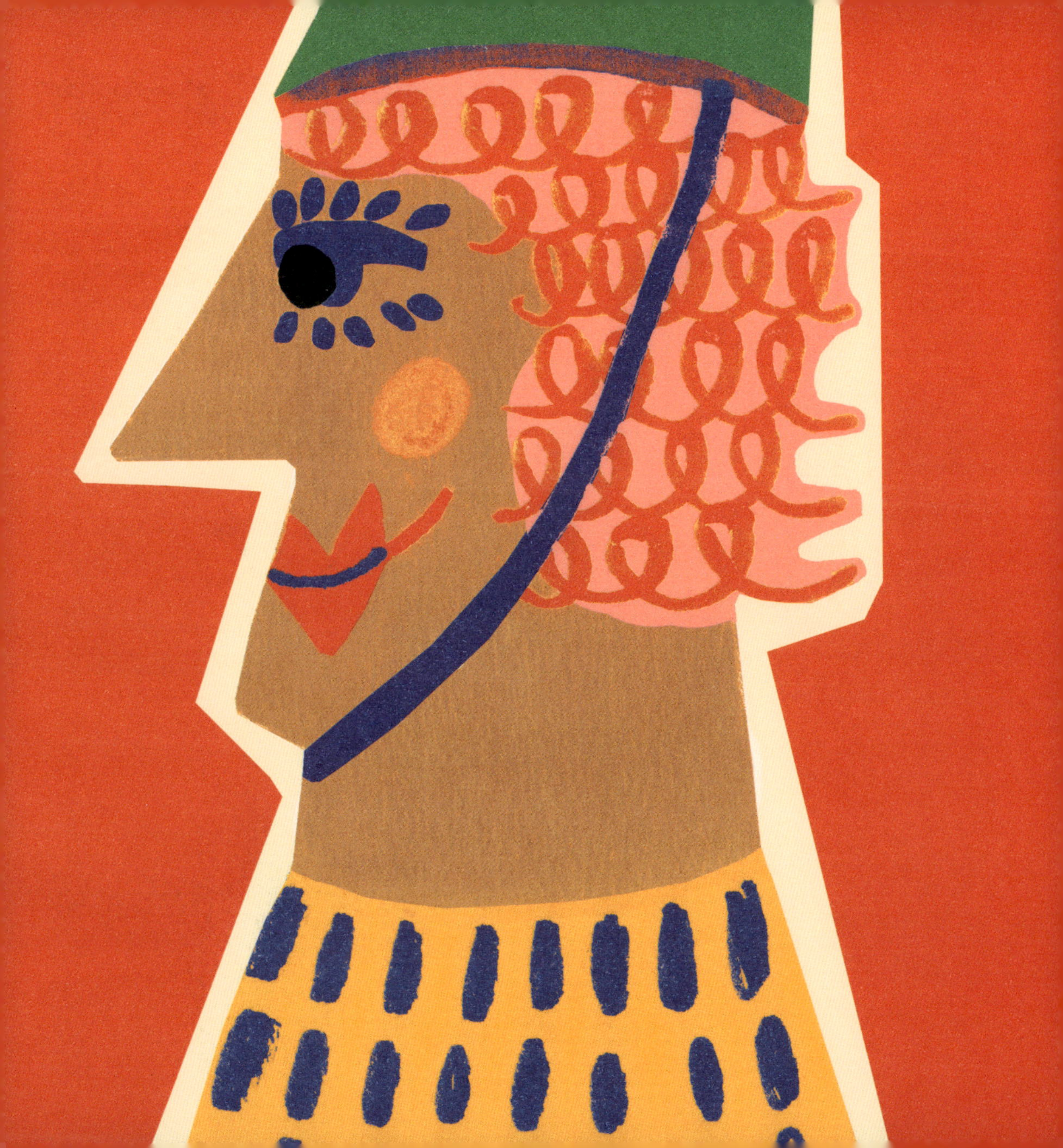

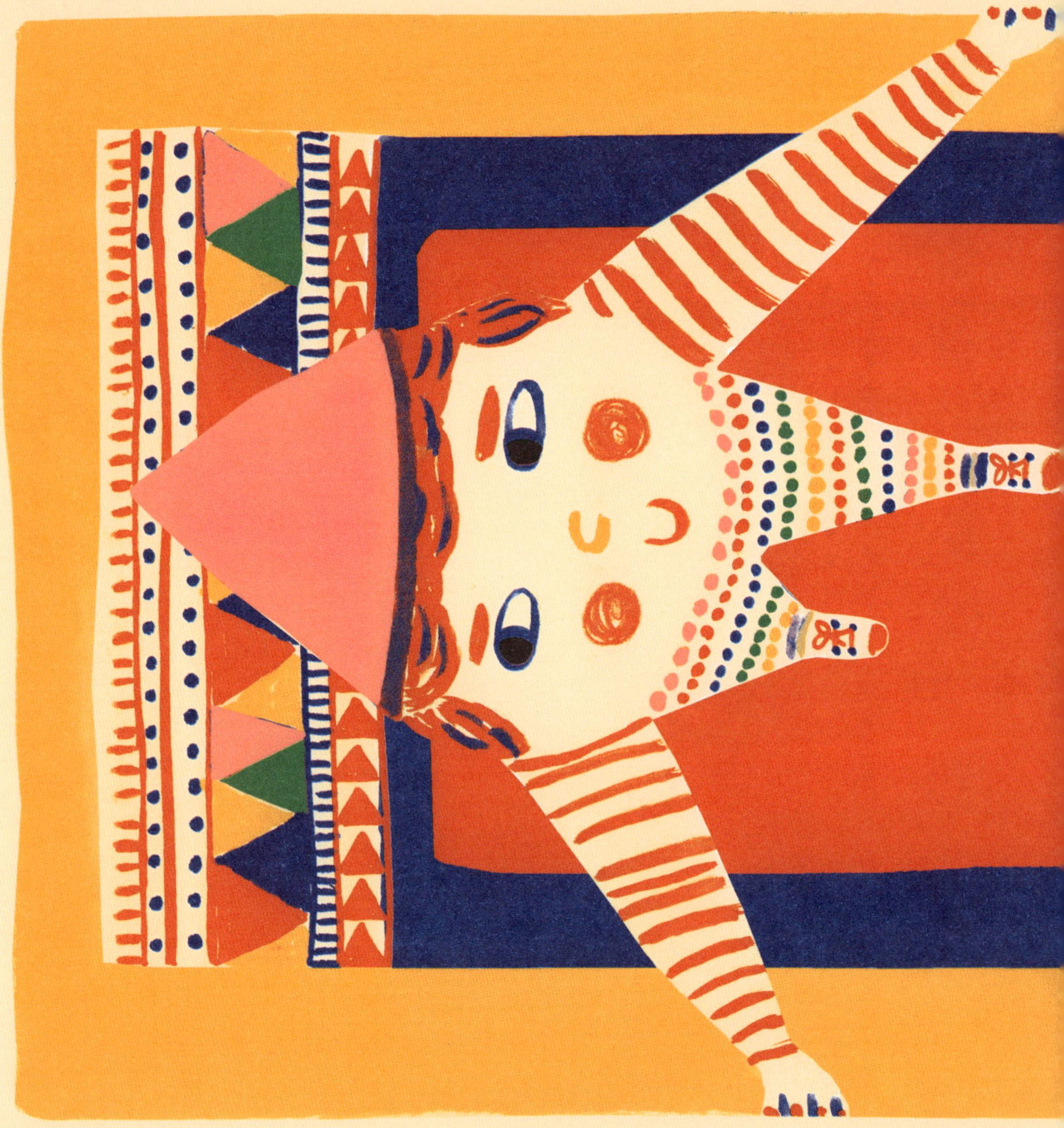

SEVEN LITTLE STEPS,
JUST LIKE A BULL.
GRANDPA SHOUTED,
"THAT'S WONDERFUL!"

EIGHT LITTLE STEPS,
LIKE A GIANT BIRD.

AUNTIE SAID, "LOOK WHAT YOU'VE LEARNED!"

NINE LITTLE STEPS,
LIKE AN ELEPHANT.
COUSIN SAID,
"GO AS FAR AS YOU WANT!"

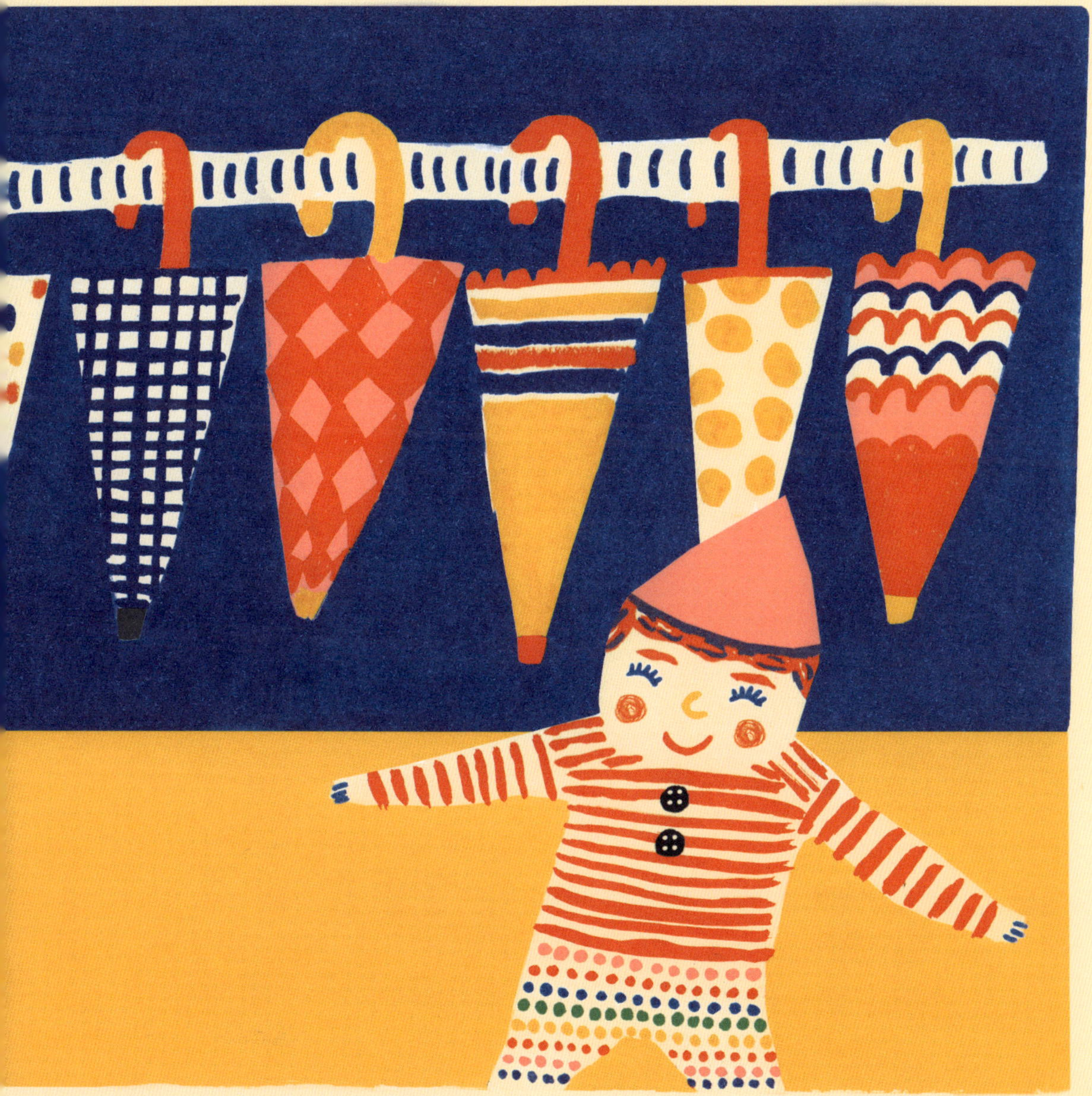

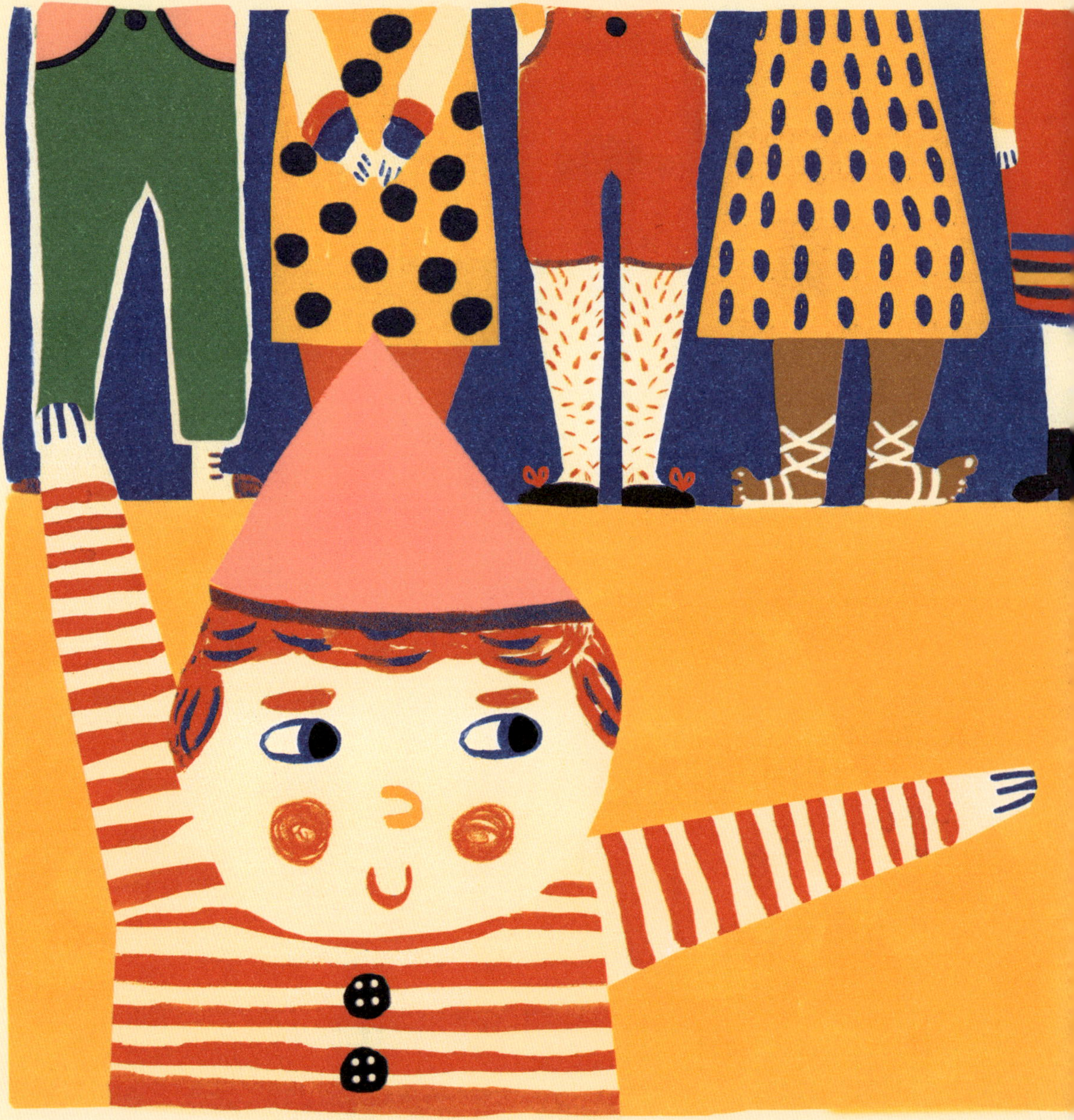

TEN LITTLE STEPS, JUST LIKE A TODDLER.
ALL THE WORLD IS MINE TO CONQUER!
AND NOW I WANT TO TAKE A RUN...

INTO YOUR ARMS

FOR A GREAT BIG HUG!!!

TINO FREITAS

Tino Freitas is a journalist, musician, writer, and story-teller. He fell in love with working for and with children as a reading mediator with the project "Roedores de Livros" (Bookworms), named one of Brazil's Best Reading Incentive Programs in 2011 by the National Foundation for Children's and Young People's Books (FNLIJ). His books feature humor alongside social criticism, and he enjoys experimenting with how books themselves, as physical objects, can help convey a story.

To learn more about Tino's work, visit http://literatino.blogspot.com

JANA GLATT

Jana Glatt is a designer and holds a graduate degree in children's book illustration. She became fascinated with creating characters and settings when she was studying theater. Her work was included in the 6th Ibero-American Catalogue of Illustration, with exhibits in Guadalajara, Mexico, and Bologna, Italy. She used water color, acrylics, and colored pencils to illustrate this book.

To learn more about Jana's work, visit http://cargocollective.com/janaglatt